Tracking & Hunting
Ruumiya

Margaret James

Illustrated by **Jesse Young**

*This book is dedicated to the beautiful, lively **Sophie**, **Ruby** and **Joey Young**.*
Thank you for inspiring your daddy to create such fun pictures!

Thank you to **Daisy Tjupamtarri Ward**, **Margaret KemarreTurner OAM**,
Benedict Kngwarraye Stevens, **Marjorie Nyunga Williams**
and the knowledgeable students who shared their goanna tracking and hunting stories with us,
especially **Jess**, **Stanley**, **Walter**, **Valentine**, **Alberto**, **Javen**, **Tyson**, **Eva** and **Christiana**.

READING
Tracks

It is winter in the Western Desert, real cold.
The land is dry and the grass is long.

In this desert country, the grasses, bushes and mulga trees don't cover all of the ground. There are big patches of red sand in between the plants.

We go hunting out bush in my aunty's troopie –
my big sister, my cousin, our little dog and me.
We take a crowbar, a shovel, matches and water.

Can you see the thorny devil?

3

We walk through the dry bush and over the red sand.
Sharp spinifex grass brushes against our legs.

Our little dog helps us to look for a mound of sand, or
marks in the dirt, where a goanna might have been digging.
We call goannas ruumiya in our Luritja language.

We can't see goanna tracks, because
the goannas are all hiding from the
cold. They aren't walking about, leaving
tracks on the sand. But we see big
camel tracks on the sand.

We look for signs of a **goanna hole.** When we
see something, we **tap** the ground with the
crowbar, listening for a hollow sound.

We search for a hollow **funnel** under the
ground, where the goannas are hiding.

We **dig** in a hole near a tree, but there are
no goannas in that one.

We walk further into the bush and try more
holes, but we find **no goannas.**

We walk a long way through the bush. Suddenly my big sister calls out,

"'Ey, I found something"!

She shows us a heap of sand, and when she taps on the ground next to the sand heap with the crowbar, we hear the hollow sound.

Big sister starts to dig out the mound of sand with her crowbar. Then she uses the shovel to get deeper into the narrow tunnel. When she gets really deep into the tunnel, and she knows she is close to a goanna, she chucks the shovel on the dirt and digs with her hands.

Can you see the thorny devil?

When she feels a goanna, she grabs its tail and pulls it out of the hole. The goanna is sleeping because it is winter, and its body slows down in the cold.

The first one she pulls out is a baby. Big sister gives it to me to hold so that the dog doesn't bite it.

Then she finds a big one in the same tunnel and she pulls it out by its tail. I put the baby goanna back in the hole because we don't eat the baby ones.

can you see the thorny devil?

Big sister holds the goanna by the tail
and hits its head on the hard ground to kill it.

The little dog gets excited and tries to bite it too.

Big sister sits down on the dirt and breaks the goanna's legs.
Then she pushes sand against the bottom of the goanna's stomach
area. She uses the sand to help her grip the guts, or intestines.

She pulls the guts out slowly. It looks like a long sausage.
Big sister buries the guts when it is all out of the goanna.

can you see the thorny devil?

Me and my cousin go to collect firewood and we start the fire.

We yarn around the fire while we wait for the big, hot flames to burn down into coals. Then we bury the goanna under the hot coals and ashes to cook.

can you see the thorny devil?

After a long time, the goanna is cooked and we pull it out of the fire.
We pull it apart and break it up.

We all like the fat the best, so we share that.
Then we eat the meat. It tastes real good!

Ruumiya, yum!

can you see the thorny devil?

We light the long, dry grass before we leave, so it will burn down and clear the country for us to see the goannas' burrows better next time.

We drive back home in my aunty's troopie after a good time out bush.

Library For All is an Australian non-profit organisation with a mission to make knowledge accessible to all via an innovative digital library solution.

Visit us at libraryforall.org
Email us at info@libraryforall.org

Tracking and Hunting Ruumiya

This edition published 2021 by Library For All, Ltd

© Margaret James, 2018–2021

Previously published by Honey Ant Readers

Honey Ant® Readers (Pty) Ltd
PO Box 3042 Wooli, NSW 2462
ABN: 18 164 267 047
Website: www.honeyant.com.au
Email: info@honeyant.com.au

Illustrations by Jesse Young

A catalogue record for this book is available from the National Library of Australia

ISBN 978-1-922591-77-7
SKU01275

CPSIA information can be obtained
at www.ICGtesting.com
Printed in the USA
BVRC100903140621
609527BV00011B/263

* 9 7 8 1 9 2 2 5 9 1 7 7 7 *